THE
GANG

THE GANG

A story about bullying

by

Mick Gowar

W

FRANKLIN WATTS

NEW YORK • LONDON • SYDNEY

First published in 1995 by Franklin Watts

This paperback edition published in 1998

Franklin Watts
96 Leonard Street
London EC2A 4RH

Franklin Watts Australia
14 Mars Road
Lane Cove
NSW 2066

A CIP catalogue record for this book
is available from the British Library

ISBN 0 7496 3283 6 (pbk)
      0 7496 2024 2 (hbk)

Dewey Classification 362.7

Printed in Great Britain

Foreword

Some people spend loads of money trying to look
different. Fashion designers and hairdressers make their
living giving people individual style. There comes a time
in many people's lives when they want to stand out
from the crowd; want to be seen as special; want to
show the rest of the world they're independent.

This is a phase which comes from feeling
confident and comfortable with who you are, or else
from feeling rebellious and wanting to challenge
establishment, parents, bosses and whoever else might
notice.

Most of the time though, most of us feel a bit shy,
a bit scared and a bit self conscious. We want to fit in.
We want people to notice us, but in a low-profile sort of
way. It's nice to be popular but not too popular.

Some people stand out from the crowd through
no fault of their own. Being fat, thin, tall, short, black,
white, yellow, spotty, hairy, bald, smelly, clever, dim,
'too weird' or 'too normal' can cause problems. If you
are 'too' anything, you run the risk of being noticed.

Often what happens at school if you get noticed, is

bullies pick on you. In a strange way, bullies want what you've got. They want to be noticed. They want attention. Even if it's only from people being afraid of them. Bullies pick on people because it gives them a feeling of power.

Bullies get off on power. And what gives bullies the most power, is silence. If someone is being bullied and they don't report what's happening then the bully gets away with it. Often, he gives someone a hard time and everyone else around keeps quiet because they're scared if they blab they'll get bullied.

People who are bullied often keep quiet because they feel embarrassed. They hope if they keep quiet, the bully will go away and pick on someone else. Trouble is, if a bully gets away with it, he'll go on doing it.

To stop bullies, you have to take away their power. Silence is what gives them power.

Schools can be very cruel places. But so can the rest of the world. Even if you don't want to stand out, maybe you do. Maybe bullies pick on you because you're a target. Fair enough. Being different is something you might be very happy about some of the time. Being a target is not a problem as long as you don't become a victim.

If someone gives you stick. Speak. Talk. Tell. Inform. Explain. Describe. Announce. Blab. Don't keep quiet.

Bullies thrive on quiet.

In this book, and in all the agony columns in all the magazines, whenever bullying is mentioned, 'quiet' is a dirty word.

Nick Fisher
Just Seventeen

One

"No more arguing," said Mum, holding out the shorts. "Just put them on. You're going to school, not to a fashion show. I don't know why you're making such a fuss. It's only for one day. Your jeans will be dry by tomorrow."

Lucy gazed at the shorts. She felt the sharp, insistent itch as tears of frustration tried to claw their way out from behind her eyes. The shorts were stupid, horrible, revolting! They weren't lycra cycling shorts or cut-downs, they were the sort of shorts which scoutmasters in cartoon films wear - baggy, khaki; a joke, a horrible joke. What would Natalie say if she went to school wearing them?

"I can't stand here all morning," Mum snapped. "I've got breakfast to cook. There's nothing else to wear, so you might as well get used to it, my girl. I paid good money for those shorts, and I'm not seeing it go to waste."

Mum turned and stalked out of the room before Lucy could reply, leaving the traces of her bad temper behind her, like a sharp, unpleasant scent.

Lucy gazed down at the disgusting shorts lying on the bed. They looked like the discarded cocoon of some nightmarish creature.

Maybe Natalie would understand, would sympathise and say: "Aren't mums the pits! The things they make you wear! Cheer up! Here, have some chocolate . . ." And put her arm round Lucy's shoulder. Maybe . . . maybe . . .

It wouldn't be so bad, thought Lucy, if yesterday hadn't been such a good day. Hardly a single sharp word. She'd even been the baby when they'd played Mums and Dads – and that was the role everybody wanted. If only every day could be like that. Lucy felt hot tears welling up again.

Lucy crept down the road that led to Highfield Junior school, keeping as close to the thick privet hedges as she could. If only I could be invisible, she thought. If only I could blink my eyes or snap my fingers, and today turned into tomorrow, and I was wearing my jeans and everything was all right again.

She turned the corner and stopped suddenly. Up ahead were Gayle and Stephanie, two other members of Natalie's gang. Lucy backed into the hedge, praying they wouldn't look round and see her. She could hear them laughing as they strolled up the road. Not a care in the world, thought Lucy with a pang of jealousy.

She heard heavy footsteps behind her. Clare was walking slowly up the road towards her. Oh no! thought Lucy. Fat, frumpy Clare, with carroty hair and freckles, who nobody liked – well, nobody that mattered; nobody who was in Natalie's gang. No wonder, thought Lucy. What has she got on?

Clare was wearing a frock – there was no other word for it – and it was shocking pink and covered with tiny poisonous-looking yellow flowers. The ruffles at the collar and the slight but noticeable difference in the lengths of the sleeves announced to the world that it had been made by an incompetent, amateur dressmaker with no colour sense.

If I had to wear that, thought Lucy, I'd refuse to go to school! But Clare didn't seem to mind. She was strolling along swinging her arms as if she didn't care what she looked like. She stopped when she saw Lucy, who was still cowering in the hedge.

"Are you all right?" asked Clare.

Lucy didn't answer.

Clare didn't seem to mind. "You'll have to hurry up," she added. "The bell'll be going in a minute."

Lucy turned her back on Clare and stared in the opposite direction. No one in Natalie's gang ever spoke to Clare, ever. Natalie had even led a chant of "We hate Clare" in the playground a couple of weeks ago. The strange thing was that Clare hadn't seemed at all bothered. She'd just shrugged and walked away. They'd carried on chanting, though, until Mrs Williams had come all the way out to the playground from the staff-room and asked them to stop.

"Are you coming?" persisted Clare.

Lucy still ignored her.

Clare shrugged and continued walking doggedly up the road.

Lucy waited a moment or two and then looked round. Good! she thought. Gayle and Stephanie were no longer in sight. Taking a deep breath, she continued her crab-like progress towards the school gates.

Lucy sidled round the tall concrete gatepost. She had her hands clamped firmly to her sides to try and stop the voluminous legs of the shorts flapping too much as she walked.

The gang was in a tight circle by the gate. Lucy crept towards the little group. Natalie was telling a joke.

'What's the difference between a buffalo and a bison?"

"Dunno . . . What?" came a chorus of voices.

There was a tension about the group, even though all the girls were smiling and some had already begun chuckling.

"You can't wash yer 'ands in a buffalo," announced Natalie in a forced stage-cockney accent, "can yer!!"

There was an immediate gale of laughter led by Natalie herself. Lucy did her best to join in.

As if by instinct, Natalie turned towards Lucy, and stopped laughing. As if on cue, the rest of the laughter died away. Natalie's eyes shone with delight as she pointed at Lucy.

"What have you got on?" she demanded, pointing at Lucy's shorts. Lucy blushed scarlet.

No one moved or spoke.

"Yeckkgh!!" exclaimed Natalie.

Stephanie was the first to follow Natalie's lead. "What a state!" she bellowed. The whole group at once began howling with exaggerated laughter. Lucy turned and fled towards the toilets, careless of whether the shorts flapped or not, and pursued by the shrieks and jeers of her friends.

TWO

When Lucy got into the classroom, Natalie, Stephanie and Gayle were already sitting in their places at the table by the big window. But there was no room left for Lucy. Carly was sitting in Lucy's usual place, next to Natalie. Lucy felt a horrible sinking feeling in her stomach.. As she walked passed the table trying not to look, a foot snaked out and Lucy sprawled forward in the gangway just as Mrs Williams came into the room. There was a gale of laughter from Natalie's table.

Mrs Williams sighed wearily. She felt exhausted, even though the day had hardly begun.

"You should look where you're going, Lucy," she said in a tired voice. "Sit down."

Lucy picked herself up. Her right knee was grazed; she tried desperately not to cry.

Lucy looked round. There were no places left, except . . .

"Hurry up, Lucy," said Mrs Williams. "There's a place there - beside Clare." She pointed to the empty chair on the table in the dark corner of the room, near the door that led to the big sinks and the toilets.

There was a snort and a suppressed giggle from Natalie's table as Lucy walked slowly down the gap between the tables and sat down heavily next to Clare.

"I do wish you wouldn't keep changing places," complained Mrs Williams, and sighed again. She opened the register:

"Michael . . ?"

"Here, miss."

"Adrian . . ?"

"Yes, miss."

Lucy shuffled her chair to one side so that she was sitting as far away from Clare as possible.

Mrs Williams looked up. "I do wish you wouldn't make that horrible scraping noise," she said. She looked down at the register again.

"Peter . . ?"

There was a silence.

"Peter . . ?" she repeated.

Another silence.

"Does anyone know where Peter is?"

No one replied.

"Absent," said Mrs Williams to no one in particular, putting down her blue pen and drawing a circle in red next to Peter's name.

"William . . ?"

But before William could speak, Peter burst through the door.

"Sorry I'm late, miss," he gasped, "only my dad's car wouldn't start."

Mrs Williams gave an enormous sigh. "It's no good, no good at all - I've marked you absent now, Peter. And in ink, too." She pushed her fingers through her short, coarse grey-brown hair. "I'll have to cross it out. Oh dear - it'll look such a mess."

The hissed whispers which had been going on since Mrs Williams began the register had now swollen into outbreaks of conversation.

Mrs Williams sighed again. "I do wish you could be quiet while I'm taking the register," she said. But no one seemed to be paying attention.

When registration was over, the class lined up for assembly. Lucy found herself at the back of the row, immediately behind Clare. Natalie, Stephanie, Gayle and Carly were at the front.

"In twos, Lucy," Mrs Williams reminded her wearily.

Reluctantly, Lucy moved up until she was standing beside Clare. She heard a snort and a giggle from the front of the line. She looked up to see Natalie, Stephanie, Gayle and Carly gloating at her.

"Please be quiet going into the hall," implored Mrs Williams.

The whispering crocodile trooped along the low, narrow corridor and into the hall. They were the last class to arrive, and they took their places at the back.

"Hymn number sixty-three," announced Mr Bottomley, the headmaster, "O God, our help in ages past."

He nodded towards the piano where Mrs Williams was now sitting, peering at a crumpled sheet of music as if it was a toxic fungus. She selected a chord that was somewhere between a ninth and a nightmare, and the whole school lurched into the first verse:

"O God, our help in ages past,

Our hope for years to come . . ."

All except for Natalie, Stephanie, Gayle and Carly who were standing behind Lucy.

"Oh, God! Have you seen Lucy's shorts?" sang Natalie.

"Yes aren't they really gross!" responded Stephanie.

"We don't want someone dressed like that," continued Natalie, "to be a friend of ours."

Up until that moment Lucy had still hoped that Natalie might change her mind, that somehow she could convince Natalie that it hadn't been her fault. But she knew Natalie's tactics too well; she'd seen how Natalie would pick out a fresh victim and how she would signal to the gang how they were supposed to behave. It was all so familiar - and so final. Today, Lucy knew, the victim would be her, and there was nothing she could do about it.

Lucy felt a black wave of helplessness and misery engulf her. She could restrain herself no longer. She bent her head and let the tears roll down her cheeks and plop on to the open hymn book in her hands.

Three

Lucy stared across the playground to the small knot of girls playing by the low wall that separated the grey tarmac from the school field. Between Lucy and the gang, a large mob of boys whooped and yelled and chased a plastic football from one end of the playground to the other.

Despite the European Cup Second Round Replay that separated them, Lucy could see Natalie and Stephanie sitting next to each other on the wall. Gayle was sitting a few metres away doing an elaborate mime with her hands, as if she was either assembling or dismantling a highly complicated machine. Carly was on all fours at Natalie's and Stephanie's feet. As if she suddenly realised she was there, Natalie grabbed Carly round the waist and hauled her up and on to her lap. Lucy could see Natalie's mouth making cooing sounds as she petted and cuddled Carly.

Lucy felt a sharp stab of jealousy. She looked around the playground. There must be someone else she could play with.

In the opposite corner to Natalie's gang, a small group of girls from the class below Lucy's were playing with Sylvanian animals. Secretly Lucy would have loved to join in with them. She glanced quickly over to the group around Natalie. She remembered how Natalie had sneered about Sylvanians on the single occasion that she had consented to come round to Lucy's house to stay the night.

"You don't like those, do you?" Natalie had asked, almost as soon as she had entered Lucy's bedroom.

"No, of course not!" Lucy had lied.

Natalie had looked round the room, noting the lock keeper's cottage and river barge which Lucy had meticulously tidied and put on the windowsill ready. The sleep-over had not been a success.

Lucy gazed wistfully at the third years, clustered around their imaginary woodland homestead.

Then she looked at the gang playing in their imaginary home - Mum, Dad, Baby . . . She looked back at the Sylvanians. What if she just went up to them and asked them if she could join in? Then she looked back to where the gang were playing. What would Natalie say if she saw Lucy playing with third years? Lucy shuddered. No, she couldn't risk it.

Lucy glanced at her watch. Another ten minutes to go.

The side door of the school building opened and Mrs Williams carefully backed out. Although it was a warm day, she was huddled up in a thick beige coat with faded brown and green plaid collar and cuffs. She had a whistle on a piece of red braid round her neck and was clutching a coffee mug in both hands. She looked slowly round the playground, took a sip of coffee, and grimaced.

Lucy noticed Clare bending down under the tall oak tree that grew by the gate. She was picking up acorns.

Lucy's mood lifted a little. At least I'm not like Clare, she thought. At least I usually have someone to play with. Clare never...

But before Lucy could complete the thought, an enormous blow on her back knocked the air from her lungs and threw her to the ground. Lucy lay on the ground unable to breathe, unable to cry. A small circle of children stared down at her as she lay on the ground gasping. As the first breaths were sucked into her lungs, Lucy began to cry. It wasn't simply because of the shock and pain of the blow, Lucy was also crying for the friends she had lost and the games she couldn't play.

As her sobs were at last beginning to subside, Lucy heard a familiar weary voice: "Could you stand aside, please, children. She may be hurt."

Mrs Williams looked down at Lucy.

"Are you all right, Lucy?" she asked. "What happened, did you fall over or something?"

"N-n-no, M-Mrs W-w-williams," gasped Lucy. "Something knocked me over."

Mrs Williams bent down, and with a heavy sigh picked up the football that was still lying beside Lucy. "Oh dear," she moaned. "How many times must you boys be told? Play with soft balls or tennis balls. Someone could get badly hurt. I'm confiscating this ball until the end of the day. Come and see me in my room at half past three . . ."

Mrs Williams was interrupted by the sound of an electric bell ringing inside the school building. "Line up in twos," she said. She held out a limp hand to help Lucy to her feet. "Come on, Lucy," she said, "you'll soon be feeling better, won't you . . ."

Lucy clambered to her feet. She was still trembling from the shock of being knocked over, and from her crying.

Lucy was surrounded by the circle of children which always gathers around a playground accident or a fight. Some were simply curious, some were ghoulishly hoping to see a serious injury like the time when Peter, now in Class Four but then in Class One, had fallen out of the oak tree, even though climbing it was strictly forbidden. It was now one of the school legends:

"His leg bone stuck right out through the skin," trembling Infants would be told in hushed tones. "And there was pints and pints of blood everywhere. And if Mr Bottomley hadn't called an ambulance he would have died - honest!"

As Lucy was led through the circle by Mrs Williams she saw Clare, who looked genuinely concerned, and Natalie who looked at Lucy with icy contempt.

The circle of children began to disperse as it became clear that nothing really exciting had happened. But from behind her, Lucy heard Natalie's voice, clear and carrying: "What a crybaby! We don't want crybabies in our gang!"

Four

"Get your Victorian projects out of your trays and carry on with them," instructed Mrs Williams. "Quietly . . ." she added, too late, as a small stampede of children rushed to the low shelving units under the windows.

Mrs Williams turned her back on the developing scrum and began to walk slowly towards the stockroom at the back of the class. She stopped when she reached the table Lucy was sitting at.

"Haven't you got your project, Lucy?" she asked. "It was about . . . er . . ." Mrs Williams squinted lopsidedly at the ceiling as if she was hoping that the topic of Lucy's project had been spray painted on to the discoloured plasterboard. It hadn't.

"Fashion, miss," prompted Lucy.

"Oh yes, I remember now," said Mrs Williams, not entirely truthfully. "Why aren't you working on it?"

Lucy paused for a second or two before answering. "I was doing it with Natalie," she replied. "We'd just finished planning it, but we hadn't . . . er . . . actually done any writing or drawing or anything yet."

Mrs Williams looked down at Lucy in surprise and then across to Clare who was working next to Lucy. Clare was sticking the last of the pictures she'd cut from magazines on to the cover of her project. Then it would be finished. Mrs Williams looked at the intimidating pile of paper stitched between the garishly decorated cardboard covers. Clare's handwriting was very small; it would be a lot of marking. Mrs Williams groaned involuntarily. She looked back at Lucy, who was still sitting in her seat gazing at the empty half of the table in front of her.

"Well . . ?" demanded Mrs Williams. Lucy looked at her, puzzled.

"Hadn't you better start something?" suggested Mrs Williams. "Everyone else is almost finished."

Lucy glanced round the room. It was true. From the back of the room she could see Michael and Adrian. Michael was handing each page of their project to Adrian, who was punching holes in the margins and then passing them back to Michael, who was threading each page on to a thick plait of red, white and blue embroidery silk. Most people in the room were either binding their work or decorating the covers. Only Lucy and the little gang around Natalie's table at the front seemed to have no work to do.

"Well . . ?" repeated Mrs Williams.

Lucy looked up at her again.

"You're not going to get much done here, are you?" asked Mrs Williams.

"Sorry, miss . . ?"

Mrs Williams gave an exasperated sigh. "If you're supposed to be working with Natalie, you're not going to do much work if you're sitting at opposite ends of the room, are you?" Mrs Williams spoke in the clear, slow

voice she kept specially for dealing with Infants.
As Lucy stood up and began to walk slowly towards the
table of giggling girls at the front of the room, Mrs
Williams turned and recommenced her slow progress to
the stockroom.

Lucy reached the table where the rest of the gang
were sitting.

"Natalie . . ." Lucy's nerve faltered. She wished
now she hadn't started the project with Natalie.

"What do you want?" Natalie demanded. She
spoke without turning round, deliberately keeping her
back to Lucy.

"It - it's our project - er, you know, 'Victorian
Fashion'. . ."

"Oh, that -", said Natalie coldly. "I'm not doing
that any more. I'm doing 'Victorian Hairstyles' with
Carly. Her sister Sharon's a real hairdresser in this dead
glamorous salon in London - so our project's gonna be
brilliant!"

Lucy stood there, frozen to the spot. She had no
idea what to do, what to say.

All the time she'd been speaking, Natalie hadn't
turned to face Lucy, but had thrown the words carelessly
over her shoulder. Now she did turn round.

"Are you still here?" she asked. "Do you always
hang around places where you're not wanted?"

Natalie turned back to the table with a broad grin
on her face. The others in the gang took the hint and,
on cue, there came a succession of poorly suppressed

giggles and snorts.

"B-but our project on Fashion -" Lucy began,

"Fashion!! With you!" Natalie almost spat out the words. She gazed down at the shorts. "Get real!"

The other girls on the table guffawed.

"I-I c-can't help it," gulped Lucy.

Natalie turned round again. Something metal glinted in her hand. "Yes you can," she said. "And I'll show you how."

She reached out. There was a muffled snipping sound.

Lucy looked down. There was a two-inch-long scissor cut in the right leg of her shorts. Lucy gazed down in horror while raucous laughter exploded all around her. She walked back to her seat too stunned and horrified even to cry. The shorts were horrible but Mum would have a fit when she saw the scissor cut. Whatever Lucy said, Mum was sure to blame her - especially after the dreadful scene that morning.

Mrs Williams came out of the stock cupboard with all the ferocity of a tortoise's head emerging from its shell.

"Work quietly, please," she called out, just as the laughter was dying down of its own accord. She was carrying a small pad of exercise paper and made her way slowly up the opposite side of the classroom to where Lucy was sitting. When she was halfway to her desk, a hand went up.

"Yes, Adrian."

"Please, miss, I've finished."

Mrs Williams sighed. "Good," she said in a bored voice.

"Well, don't you want to see it, miss?" asked Adrian.

"Not now, Adrian," said Mrs Williams sharply. "Can't you see I'm busy? I'll collect in the projects at the end of the week, and I'll look at them all then - yours as well."

She resumed her stately progress to her desk at the front of the room. As she was sitting down, another hand went up.

"Yes, Natalie," said Mrs Williams. "What's the matter now?"

"Please, miss, I want to go to the toilet."

Mrs Williams seemed to think about this for a moment or two. "All right, Natalie," she sighed. "But don't be all day."

Lucy watched Natalie stand up and start walking towards her. She remembered what her mother had said, after the sleep-over: "You shouldn't be such a doormat, Lucy. You've got to learn to stand up for yourself. Stand up to people like Natalie. If you do what they say all the time, they'll never respect you."

Natalie walked past Lucy's table without even the briefest sideways glance. It was as if Lucy was invisible, or as if she didn't exist.

Yes, decided Lucy. Yes, I will stand up to her.

As the door closed behind Natalie, Lucy's hand

shot up.

"Yes, Lucy," said Mrs Williams wearily.

"Please, miss, can I go to the toilet?"

"Not you as well," sighed Mrs Williams. "Can't you wait until lunch time?"

"Er, no, miss."

"Oh, very well then. But hurry up."

Lucy hurried through the door, past the big sinks and into the girls' toilets.

Natalie was washing her hands but looked up when she heard Lucy's footsteps.

She turned her back on Lucy in an exaggeratedly theatrical way.

"Natalie . . ." Lucy began, and faltered. She realised that she had no idea what to say.

"Why are you following me?" demanded Natalie icily.

"I'm - I'm not . . ."

"Yes you are," Natalie snapped back. "You're always following me - and Stephanie and Gayle and Carly. And we're getting really sick of it. You're always tagging along where you're not wanted. You're so, so sad."

Lucy stood in silence, gazing at the cracked vinyl tiles under her feet while Natalie dried her hands on a green paper towel. Natalie screwed up the used towel and threw it on the floor.

"Out of my way," she commanded. "I've got to get back to class." And she pushed past Lucy. As she did so, she trod heavily on Lucy's toes.

"So sorry, I'm sure," said Natalie sarcastically. "But that's what happens when you follow people!" And she swept out of the door.

Lucy stood in front of the basins. She bit her lip, trying to force herself not to cry. The pain in her foot was bad, but Natalie's hateful words hurt far worse. It wasn't true, it just wasn't true. She didn't just hang around behind the gang. She was a proper member. She could remember two days last week when Natalie had told her that she was her best friend - her very best friend. It was on Tuesday and Wednesday. Then it was Carly who was hanging around looking miserable.

"Don't talk to Carly," Natalie had whispered. "Carly's a Durbrain!"

And they'd both laughed about it.

Lucy ran some water into the basin. It was cold, but for once it didn't matter. She splashed her red-rimmed eyes and dried them. Then she turned and walked back into the classroom.

"Where have you been, Lucy?" asked Mrs Williams, as Lucy slid into the seat beside Clare. Lucy heard sniggering coming from Natalie, Stephanie, Gayle and Carly on the front table. "I was beginning to get worried about you," continued Mrs Williams.

Lucy didn't answer,

"Have you started your project yet?"

Lucy shook her head. "No, miss."

The electric bell on the wall outside the classroom

shrilled the signal for lunch time.

"Well, you'll have to finish it by Friday . . ." But Mrs Williams's voice was lost in the hubbub as the children rushed to put their projects back in their plastic trays.

Five

Lucy walked into the dining hall on her own, and made her way slowly to the area of tables set aside for packed lunches.

Natalie, Gayle and Carly were already clustered round a table, whispering and giggling. There was an empty chair at their table. As Lucy walked towards the table, Natalie nudged Gayle, and when Lucy reached them, Gayle put her empty lunchbox on the seat.

"It's taken!" she trumpeted before Lucy could even ask. The gang members all giggled.

Lucy made her way slowly to a table by the window, sat down and opened her lunchbox. Inside was a tuna sandwich, a drink of apple juice in a box, a miniature packet of raisins, a packet of prawn cocktail crisps, an apple and a bar of chocolate.

Lucy was surprised. Usually Mum was very strict about what Lucy was allowed for her packed lunches: "Either crisps or chocolate, but not both . . ." (Unlike Natalie's mum who would let her have crisps and chocolate and a sweet fizzy drink too.)

Maybe, thought Lucy, Mum was feeling bad about not getting my jeans dry. That would make sense - especially as Mum had been so grumpy this morning. Mum was always brisk and snappy when she broke a promise or knew she'd let Lucy down in some way.

Lucy put the chocolate bar to one side and began to eat her lunch. She was going to save the chocolate for last.

Lucy wasn't aware, until she heard a cough behind her, that Natalie had left her table. Lucy looked up. Natalie was looking down at the table in front of Lucy. She was staring at the unopened chocolate bar.

Natalie's voice was softer than it had been all morning, but there was a sharp edge to it, as if she was angry or upset. "Don't you want to be my friend any more?" she asked.

Lucy gazed up at her, astonished. "B-but, I thought . . ." she faltered. "You said . . ."

"If you want to be my friend you should act like a friend," said Natalie in a wheedling tone. "Friends share things -" she nodded in the direction of the chocolate bar.

Lucy was still so surprised at the apparent change in Natalie that she didn't react.

"Friends - real friends - share things," repeated Natalie. "Things like chocolate," she added pointedly.

"Oh," said Lucy, "do you want a piece?"

Natalie said nothing.

"Here," said Lucy handing Natalie the bar and expecting her to break off a square.

Natalie took the bar. "It's not very big - and you've got so many friends," she said, glancing back at the table where Gayle and Carly were grinning.

Lucy felt a coldness in her stomach. She knew what was going to happen, but didn't know how to stop it.

"Such a small bar and so many friends," repeated Natalie. "Oh dear - I don't think there's going to be any left for you!" And she turned back to her table. Stephanie, Gayle and Carly hooted with laughter.

"God! She's so stupid!" Lucy heard Natalie say in what might have been meant to be a whisper, if it hadn't been so loud. "Mmmmmm!" went on Natalie loudly. "What delicious chocolate! What a shame there won't be any left for Lucy . . ."

Lucy stared hard at her lunchbox, trying to shut out the cruel laughter and trying not to cry.

She was still gazing at it when the dinner lady came round.

"Still here?" the dinner lady asked. Lucy looked up and nodded.

"You feeling poorly or something?"

Lucy shook her head.

"Well, off you go outside then," said the dinner lady briskly. "You know the rules: everybody out of the dining hall by quarter past. And I want my dinner too, and I can't have it till I've finished clearing up in here. And I can't finish clearing up if half the kids in the school are still hanging about, can I?"

Lucy looked round. She was the only one left.

"Go on -" said the dinner lady sharply.

Lucy got to her feet, picked up her lunchbox, and

plodded wearily across the dining hall to the big glass doors that led to the playground.

Lucy reached out for the door handle but stopped. She took a deep breath. She didn't know if she had the courage to face Natalie and the gang again. An idea began to form in her mind. What if she said she was ill? She could spend the afternoon in the medical room. She might even be allowed to go home. Then she remembered the cut in her shorts. No, maybe going home to face Mum would be even worse than having to face the gang.

"Didn't you hear what I said?" came a gruff voice behind her.

Lucy turned round. It was the dinner lady. She pushed past Lucy and held open the door.

"You kids nowadays, you're spoiled rotten!" she grumbled. "When I was your age I couldn't wait to get outside in the fresh air and play with my friends."

Lucy didn't reply, but continued to gaze miserably out at the playground.

"Go on!" said the dinner lady crossly "Out you go!"

Six

Lucy walked out of the glass door, down the low concrete steps, and stopped. No more than three metres from the door were the gang. They were playing a skipping game.

One end of a length of yellow plastic washing line was tied around a drainpipe. Stephanie was turning the other end, while Natalie and Gayle jumped in unison and sang. Carly stood poised, ready to run in and join the other two.

"I like coffee! I like tea!" sang Natalie and Gayle.
"I like Carly in with me . . .
C . . . A . . . R . . . L . . . Y -
Carly!"

And as her name was shouted, Carly dodged under the rope as it reached the top of its upswing, and joined the other two girls.

Lucy dithered by the step. What should she do? If she appeared to want to join in - if she so much as looked at the gang - she knew that either Natalie or one of the other gang members would sneer at her, or call her names, or do something horrible to her. Yet there they were, right outside the door to the dining hall. How could she get past them without being tormented again?

Lucy listened to the rhythmical slap-slap of the rope on the tarmac and timed her move as carefully as if she was about to rush into the whirling cage of the game.

"I don't like coffee! I don't like tea! . . ." sang Natalie and Gayle.

As the rope swung up, Lucy tried to hurry past the gang while they were too preoccupied with their game to notice her.

The chanting came to an abrupt halt.

"Ooooh! Look at her!" called out Natalie. "Little Miss Snooty! Too snooty to say hello!"

Lucy stopped dead. She could feel a cold anger building up inside her.

Natalie put on a high-pitched, whining, posh accent:

"Off to play with your snobby friend Clare - are you?

"Oooh! La-di-da! Too stuck up for the likes of us - are you?"

Lucy turned round. Natalie was on the far side of the group. Stephanie, who was closest to Lucy, sniggered and put her hand on her hip. "La-di-da!" she mimicked.

Lucy gazed into Stephanie's face - a stupid, round face with great brown cow eyes and a wide mouth twisted into an ugly sneer of contempt - and all her anger and shame came to the surface. Lucy wanted to get out of the playground, away from the gang, away from Stephanie's plump, pink, sneering face. She reached out and pushed Stephanie out of her way.

Stephanie stumbled back awkwardly, tripped over the trailing skipping rope, and sat down hard on the tarmac.

"Ummm!" yelled Natalie. "I'm telling on you! Mr Wilkinson! Mr Wilkinson! Lucy hit Stephanie! Lucy hit Stephanie for no reason! Mr Wilkinson! Tell her!"

On cue, Stephanie - who up to that moment had been sitting on the ground just looking stupid - started to wail.

Lucy looked round. Mr Wilkinson, the Class Three teacher who was on playground duty, was about fifteen metres away and closing in fast.

"What's going on here?" he asked as he reached the little group.

"It was Lucy, Mr Wilkinson," said Natalie. "She hit Stephanie - for no reason. We were just skipping, and she came up and started. Tell her, Mr Wilkinson," she repeated. "Tell her!"

"Is this true, Lucy?" asked Mr Wilkinson.

But Lucy just stood there open-mouthed at the untruthfulness, the unfairness of it all.

"Well . . ?" Mr Wilkinson prompted.

Lucy said nothing, she just stared in disbelief at Natalie.

Mr Wilkinson bent down and helped Stephanie to her feet.

"Are you all right, dear?" he asked.

Stephanie made a pathetic snivelling noise.

Mr Wilkinson turned to Lucy "I want you to apologise to Stephanie - right now!" he said sternly.

Lucy couldn't believe her ears. "But, Mr Wilkinson," she protested, "she's been saying horrible things to me all day, and all the rest of them, and at lunch they took my -"

Mr Wilkinson cut her off sharply. "I'm not interested in any of that," he snapped. "Saying is one thing, but hitting someone is quite another. Apologise to Stephanie," he commanded.

"But it's not true," Lucy protested again. "I didn't hit her, I was only -"

"Oooh, Mr Wilkinson, Lucy's telling lies!" screeched Natalie in a horrified voice, "She did hit her, she did - you saw her, didn't you?"

Mr Wilkinson stood up as straight as he could and glared at Lucy. "I will not be told fibs," he announced. "You will go and sit outside Mr Bottomley's office for the rest of the dinner break."

"But, Mr Wilkinson -"

"No more arguing, Lucy! Off you go!"

Mr Wilkinson pointed grandly towards the glass doors.

Seven

"Silent reading," announced Mrs Williams. "Put away your maths books, get your reading books from your trays, and read quietly until the bell goes."

There was a scraping of chairs as one by one the children ambled over to the shelves to get their books. There was none of the enthusiasm of the morning stampede to get the projects. It was as if the announcement of 'silent reading' had a sedative effect on the children.

Lucy looked at her watch. Twenty minutes to go. She glanced across the table at Clare. Clare was already engrossed in a book which - as far as Lucy could see didn't have any pictures at all.

Lucy wasn't used to reading books in silent reading. The gang either skimmed through old comics left in the junk modelling box or talked quietly.

Mrs Williams was usually too busy tidying away by the sinks or in the stockroom to mind — just as long as they didn't make too much noise.

Lucy looked across to where the gang were sitting. Natalie was making tiny plaits in Carly's hair. Despite everything that had happened, Lucy felt a sharp pang of jealousy.

Stephanie and Gayle were playing with a folded paper beak. Lucy knew the game well. You picked a number, then a colour which was written on one of the outside sections of the beak. Then you unfolded the paper and read the message hidden inside. It was Stephanie's turn to do the choosing. Gayle opened out the paper beak and they both read the message inside. They both giggled loudly.

"Read quietly, please," said Mrs Williams.

Stephanie and Gayle pulled exaggeratedly straight faces, then collapsed into suppressed giggles again.

Mrs Williams ignored them and got slowly to her feet.

"I'm just going to tidy up the resources area," she announced. "So I want you to be quiet until I get back." Lucy put her hand up.

"Yes, Lucy?"

"Please, miss, can I get a book from the library?"

Mrs Williams sighed. "I suppose so," she said. "But be quick, and don't disturb anyone who's trying to work in there."

Lucy stood up and walked towards the door.

As she approached Natalie's table, Stephanie leant across and showed Natalie and Carly the message on the paper beak which she and Gayle had found so funny. All four girls giggled. Then they saw Lucy. They nudged each other and laughed even louder.

"I said quietly," Mrs Williams reminded the class from the doorway at the back of the room.

Lucy shut the door of the classroom behind her and stood for a moment in the corridor. It was a relief to be away from the gang, and away from all the nudges and winks and giggles and pointed looks. She walked as slowly as she could down the long, yellow-painted corridor that led to the library.

Lucy stopped at the half-open door of Class Three. A tape was playing on the small stereo that stood on the bookshelf beside the blackboard and behind Mr Wilkinson's chair. Lucy listened for a moment. She recognised the tape, it was a Just William story that Mr Wilkinson had played to Lucy's class when they were third years. Lucy peered into the room. Mr Wilkinson was lounging across the front table in his usual pose. He was smiling, and some of the children were laughing. But not like Natalie and Stephanie and Gayle and Carly had just laughed at Lucy. This was the sort of laughing that came from enjoying something together, not the sort of laughing that's supposed to make someone else feel left out, miserable and alone.

When she was in Class Three, Lucy had thought that the music and the story tapes Mr Wilkinson had played them were really boring. She couldn't wait to be in the top class. Now she found herself wishing that she was back in Class Three, listening to the swan music or the gnome music. Even the Just William stories, which she'd really hated when she'd been in Mr Wilkinson's class, sounded much more fun than they had a year ago.

She turned away from the cheery sounds coming from Class Three and resumed her plod towards the library. Class Two's room was empty, but when she reached Class One, once again she looked into the room.

All the children were bunched together on the small square of worn beige carpet in the story corner, next to the low shelves of brightly coloured picture books. Lucy could just see Miss Ferguson's back. The children were facing her, entranced by the story she was telling them. Then Miss Ferguson held up the book she was reading from. Several children pointed excitedly at the picture she was showing them and shouted out. Miss Ferguson shushed them gently and continued with the story. Lucy crept away.

She reached the library and opened the door. The small room was full of Class Two children selecting books from the home reading section. There was a happy buzz of purposeful activity. Miss Bennett turned round when she heard the door close.

"Hullo, Lucy," she said brightly. "Is there something I can do for you?"

"I've just come in for a reading book," replied Lucy.

"Well, you'd better hurry up," said Miss Bennett, pointing at the clock. "There's only five minutes to go before home time."

Lucy glanced round the room at the busy children and felt, once again, shut out, on the edge of things.

"Er, I don't think I'll bother in that case," she said. "Thanks, Miss Bennett."

She hurried out of the library and walked briskly back down the corridor, trying to ignore the sounds of excitement coming from Class One and the laughter coming from Class Three.

Mrs Williams was back at her desk. "Oh, Lucy," she said, "I'd almost forgotten you. Did you find a book?"

Lucy shook her head.

"Oh well," sighed Mrs Williams, "I don't suppose it matters, there's only a couple of minutes to home time. Go and sit down."

Lucy walked past Natalie's table. As she did so, Natalie, Stephanie, Gayle and Carly all covered their mouths with their hands in a vain attempt to control their laughter. It was as if Lucy was the funniest thing they'd ever seen.

Lucy flopped down on the chair next to Clare.

Clare looked up from her book. "They left you something," she said to Lucy, nodding towards the gang on the front table who now appeared to be helpless with mirth. "It's one of those . . . er, things."

On the table was the folded paper beak that Stephanie and Gayle had been playing with. Lucy unfolded the paper. Inside were eight messages, but they were all about her.

"Lucy lives in a pigsty," she read. "Lucy smells like dog poo," was the next. "We all hate Lucy."

Lucy looked up towards the front table. Natalie was sitting with a big smirk on her face, while Stephanie, Gayle and Carly rocked in their seats with helpless giggles.

The bell rang, and Natalie, Stephanie, Gayle and Carly unencumbered by books - were first out of the door.

Lucy made her way slowly towards the door. She stopped at Mrs Williams's desk, screwed up the paper beak and threw it into the rubbish bin.

Eight

By the time Lucy reached the cloakroom the only person there was Clare, who was always the last out. On the floor of the cloakroom lay a PE bag, empty. A pair of shorts, a T-shirt, a familiar dark blue swimming costume, and a pair of plimsolls were scattered across the floor. Lucy bent down and slowly began gathering up her things and started to push them back into her red canvas bag.

"Here..." Lucy looked up. Clare held out her Snoopy towel.

"It was outside in the corridor."

"Thanks, Clare," said Lucy.

Clare shrugged.

Lucy hung the bag back on her peg, then looked out of the window. Although she'd taken her time walking down to the cloakroom, and had just spent several minutes picking up her games kit, Lucy could see that Natalie, Stephanie, Gayle and Carly were still in the playground. They were waiting by the gates. Lucy knew who they were waiting for. She felt tears come back into her eyes. When would they give up and leave her alone, when would they have had enough?

"Er, are you walking home?" she asked Clare.

Clare shrugged again. "I can't think of any other

way to get there," she replied.

Lucy and Clare walked side by side in silence across the playground. As they approached the gate, the gang got into a tight huddle and began whispering ostentatiously. As Lucy and Clare drew level they straightened up and all stared up at the sky as if looking for rain clouds. Then, as soon as Lucy and Clare were past, Natalie, Stephanie, Gayle and Carly let out a great peal of laughter. Lucy turned round.

"Lucy lives in a pigsty!" yelled Stephanie.

"Lucy smells like dog poo!" shrieked Gayle.

"We all hate Lucy!" screamed all four girls together, and dissolved into helpless fits of raucous laughter.

Lucy and Clare walked along the road. Apart from the occasional gulp and sniff from Lucy, they walked in silence until they reached Lucy's gate.

They stood by the gate in an even more awkward silence.

Clare pulled a sour face. "I think gangs are stupid," she said.

Lucy nodded. She looked down at her shorts and noticed the scissor cut.

"Oh no!" she groaned. "I'd forgotten about that. What am I going to tell my mum?"

Clare shrugged again. "It's up to you - but why not tell her the truth?" she suggested.

"What - do you mean about Natalie and all the gang?"

Clare nodded.

"But she'd never let me have any of them round again!"

Clare shrugged. "So . . ?"

Lucy looked at her. "Do you - do you want to come in for a bit?" she asked.

Clare thought about the offer, then shook her head.

"No thanks," she replied. "My mum's expecting me back."

"What about tomorrow?" asked Lucy.

Clare shrugged. "I don't know," she replied. "I'll have to ask my mum . .. "

There was another awkward pause.

"See you tomorrow," said Clare, beginning to walk up the road.

"Yeah, see you . . ." replied Lucy.

Lucy shut the gate behind her and walked up the concrete path to her front door. She paused on the step. She tried to imagine what Mum would say if she told her what had really happened. She shuddered. Mum would be up at the school tomorrow, first thing in the morning, demanding that something was done. It would be unbearably embarrassing. Lucy flinched at the thought of it. And Natalie and the rest of the gang would never speak to her again - or worse, chant horrible things at her every single day. Mum wouldn't be able to stop them doing that, would she?

Still not sure what she would say, Lucy took a deep breath and pressed the doorbell.

Mum answered the door.

"Hullo, love," she said cheerily. "Had a nice day at school?"

Organisations

Anti-Bullying Campaign (ABC)
10 Borough High Street
London SE1 9QQ
Tel: 0171 378 1446

Childline
Freepost 1111
London N1 0BR
Tel: 0800 1111
24-hour, free and confidential advice line to help children with a wide range of issues. They will listen, comfort and protect.

Children's Legal Centre
20 Compton Terrace
London N1 2UN
Adviceline:
0171 359 6251
Advice on the law for children.

Kidscape
152 Buckingham Palace Road
London SW1W 9TR
Tel: 0171 730 3300
Free information for parents and schools on keeping safe. Programmes also available to help teach skill that help teenagers and children deal with situations.

National Children's Bureau
8 Wakley Street
London EC1V 7QE
Tel: 0171 843 6000
Research and policy centre. Provides information on where to get help on a wide range of issues.

National Society for the Prevention of Cruelty to Children (NSPCC)
42 Curtain Road
London EC2A 3NH
Tel: 0171 825 2500
NSPCC 24-hour free Helpline: 0800 800500
Offers counselling and advice.

AUSTRALIA

Kids Help Line (free)
Tel: 008 073 008

Salvo Youth Line (free)
Tel: 1800 251 008

NEW ZEALAND

Youthline
PO Box 9300
Newmarket, Auckland
Tel: 09 376 6633

Auckland City Council Youth Services
PO Box 7107
Wellesley Street, Auckland
Tel: 09 379 8488
Offers information on a wide range of groups and organisations.

SOUTH AFRICA

Child Emergency Service
Tel: 08001 23321
Free 24-hour service. They give advice on a wide range of subjects and can refer you to other relevant organisations.

Books

The following are suitable for 8- to 12-year-olds

FICTION FOR CHILDREN

Bullies at School by Theresa Breslin (Blackie Snappers)
The Present Takers by Aidan Chambers (Mammoth)
Bully by Yvonne Coppard (Red Fox)
The Bully by Jan Needle (Hamish Hamilton)

OTHER BOOKS

What Do You Know About Bullying by Pete Sanders (Franklin Watts)
This Book looks at bullying from a personal as well as a social perspective.
Storylines about children coping with bullying are illustrated in strip form
and are accompanied by clear, 'reader-friendly' texts, which provide insights
into how social problems develop, and explain what to do if the reader finds
him- or herself in a similar situation.

Don't Pick On Me by Rosemary Stones (Piccadilly Press)
This book discusses why some people bully, why others are bullied and what
you can do to change things.